Praise for the Observer

'Delightfully mad'
Telegraph

'Gigglingly delightful'
Daily Mail

'This animal-rhyming silliness goes
from strength-to-strength'
Guardian

'Colourful, witty and silly'
BookTrust

To Marble K.G.

For cat-mad Dad, Chester and Dillon J.F.

HODDER CHILDREN'S BOOKS
First published in hardback in Great Britain in 2017
by Hodder and Stoughton
This paperback edition published in 2018

A CIP catalogue record for this book
is available from the British Library.

ISBN: 978 1 444 93252 2

10 9 8 7 6 5 4 3 2 1

Printed and bound in China

MIX
Paper from
responsible sources
FSC® C104740

Hodder Children's Books
An imprint of Hachette
Children's Group
Part of Hodder and Stoughton
Carmelite House
50 Victoria Embankment
London, EC4Y 0DZ

An Hachette UK Company
www.hachette.co.uk
www.hachettechildrens.co.uk

www.kesgray.com
www.jimfield.co.uk

Oi CAT!

Hodder
Children's
Books

Written by
Kes Gray

Illustrated by
Jim Field

"Oi CAT!

Step away from
the gnat!"
said the frog.

"But I hate gnats," said the cat. "Gnats are all **gnasty** and **gnibbly** and they keep biting me on the bottom!"

"Why do you keep sitting on them, then?" asked the dog. "Why don't you sit on a **mat** instead?"

"Because the frog's changed the rules," sighed the cat. "Remember?"

"That's right," smiled the frog, "I've changed the rules.

Dogs used to sit on **frogs,** but now they sit on **logs.**

And **cats** used to sit on **mats**, but now they sit on **gnats!**"

"It's a shame
you're not a **pony**,"
said the dog.
"If you were a pony
you could sit on some
macaroni."

"Just my luck,"
sighed the cat.

"Macaroni won't nibble your bottom," said the dog.

"Will you stop talking about my bottom," said the cat.
"My bottom is none of your business!"

"If you were a **chick** you could sit on a **brick**," smiled the frog.

"If you were a **vole** you could sit on a **bowl**.

If you were a **leech** you could sit on a **peach**.

If you were a **duck** you could sit on a **truck**!"

"Well, I'm not a chick, am I?" frowned the cat.
"Or a vole, or a leech, or a duck."

"You're a **cat,**" said the dog.

"On a **gnat,**" smiled the frog.

"And rules are rules."

"If you were a **lark** you could sit on a **shark,**" said the frog.

"Unbelievable," said the cat.

"If you were a **shrimp** you could sit on a **chimp**," said the dog.

"If you were a **bunny** you could sit on some **honey**.

If you were a **pheasant** you could sit on a **present**.

If you were a **troll** you could sit on a **doll!**"

"Whatever he sits on, it has to rhyme with cat," said the frog.

"Perhaps you could sit on a **bat!**" said the dog. "Instead of a mat or a gnat, you could sit on a cricket bat, or a baseball bat, or a softball bat!"

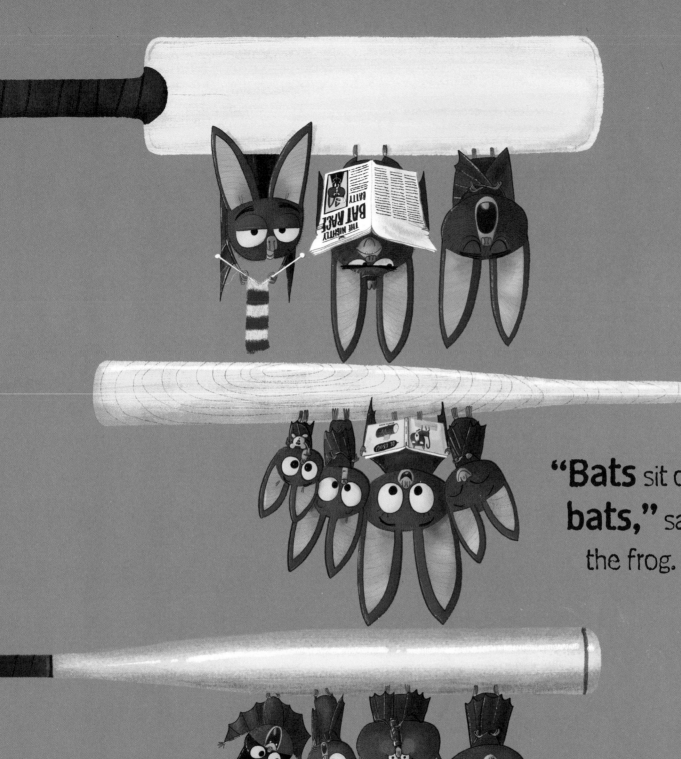

"**Bats** sit on **bats**," said the frog.

"What if you were a kitty instead of a cat?" said the dog.

"If you were a **kitty** you could sit on something **pretty** – like a pretty flamingo or some sparkly bows or some lovely colourful streamers!"

"**Dingoes** sit on **flamingos**,

crows sit on **bows**,

and **lemurs** sit on **streamers**," said the frog.

"How about a **mog?**" said the dog.
"If you were a **mog** you could sit on a **clog**. Or a **cog!**"

"Hogs sit on **clogs,"** said the frog.

"AND **cogs,** when there's a shortage of **clogs."**

"Wait a moment," smiled the cat,

"if I was a **mog** I could sit on a... "

"Step away from the **frog!**"
frowned the frog.

"Yes, no one can sit on a
frog," nodded the dog.
"It has to be something that
rhymes with frog. Or mog
or clog or cog."

DOG!

said the dog.
"Dog rhymes with
frog, mog, clog
AND COG!"

"So it does!" smiled the cat.

"So it does!"
clapped the frog.

The laughter never ends with
Oi FROG AND FRIENDS